The Boss Dog of Blossom Street

RITA RAY

Illustrated by Susan Scott

Oxford University Press

Oxford University Press, Great Clarendon Street, Oxford OX2 6DP

Oxford New York
Athens Auckland Bangkok Bogota Buenos Aires
Calcutta Cape Town Chennai Dar es Salaam
Delhi Florence Hong Kong Istanbul Karachi
Kuala Lumpur Madrid Melbourne Mexico City
Mumbai Nairobi Paris São Paulo Singapore
Taipei Tokyo Toronto Warsaw

and associated companies in
Berlin Ibadan

Oxford is a trade mark of Oxford University Press

Printed in Hong Kong

Illustrations by Susan Scott

1

Snap was a small black and brown dog. He was the boss dog of Blossom Street.

One Saturday morning he walked up and down Blossom Street as usual.

He sniffed all the doorsteps and lamp
posts. He wagged his tail at all the children
who saved scraps for him. He poked his head
into baby Kelly's pram. Kelly laughed and
touched Snap's wet nose.

4

Then Snap made sure that the dogs and
cats on the street were in their places. Dogs
had to stay in their own back yards and cats
had to sit on the back yard walls. That's if
they dared to come out at all.

Snap trotted back to his own door.
Everything seemed fine on Blossom Street.
But everything was not fine.

Snap's owners, Ada and Harry, were at home. This was odd. They always went to work on Saturday mornings. There were boxes everywhere. Harry was taking a bed apart. Ada was putting cups into a box.

'Hello, Snap,' she said, as he came in.
Snap sniffed the boxes. 'You'd better have
your Doggy Chunks before the van comes.'

'What van?' Snap thought. He soon found
out. A big van came to the front of the
house. Two men helped Harry and Ada to
put all their things in the van.

'I can't move away!' thought Snap. 'Who's going to look after Blossom Street? Who will play with the children and keep the other dogs off the street? Who will make sure the cats stay on the back yard walls?'

'Come on, Snap,' called Harry. 'Say goodbye to Blossom Street.' He picked Snap up and put him in the front of the van.

The children on Blossom Street came out to
wave as the van set off. Kelly's mum gave
Snap a bit of cake.

As he looked out of the van window Snap
thought, 'If I move away, how can I do my
job? I'm the boss dog of Blossom Street, but I
can't stay behind. I can't leave Ada and
Harry. Dogs stay with their owners. Not like
some cats I know. They'll go anywhere for a
warm fire.'

2

The van had to go slowly all the way to the new house. There was a big orange bus in front of it. Snap watched the bus and it gave him an idea. By the time he got to the new house he had a plan.

The plan could help him to be boss dog of
Blossom Street, even if he didn't live there
any more.

Snap felt a bit happier when he jumped
out of the van. He went to sniff every corner
of his new home.

The next day was Sunday and Ada and
Harry had to unpack things. The new house
had a garden at the back instead of a yard.

'The dogs round here stay in their own gardens,' Ada told Snap. 'There's no strutting about being boss dog. I'll take you for a walk later.'

Snap went to see what was at the end of the garden and he heard a yapping sound. Something was trying to get through the fence. It was a little Yorkie dog with a red ribbon tied in a bow on top of its head.

Snap couldn't believe it. 'Ugh!' he thought. 'What a wimp! That's not a *real* dog! They wouldn't have a dog like that on Blossom Street.'

He didn't even bother to bark at the little dog. He heard its owner call, 'Foofoo, Foofoo pie! Come to mummy.'

'Yuk!' thought Snap. 'Let me get back to Blossom Street.'

On Monday morning Harry and Ada went
to work. 'I've left a key next door,' said Ada
to Snap. 'Foofoo's owner will let you out in
the garden, and we'll be home at five
o'clock.'

'Will you stop talking to that dog as if he
understands?' said Harry.

'What do you mean? Of course he
understands, don't you, Snap?' said Ada.

Later, Foofoo's owner unlocked the door into the garden.

'Good,' thought Snap.

He ran into the garden and started to dig a hole.

'Bad doggie,' called Foofoo's owner. 'Don't teach my little Foofoo bad tricks.'

Snap tried to talk to the dog on the other
side. He was a large bulldog with droopy
eyes.

'This looks better,' thought Snap. He
barked in a friendly way. But the big dog
said nothing at all.

'I can't stand this much longer,' thought
Snap. 'I must try to get back to Blossom
Street.'

That night he fell asleep thinking of his plan for keeping his eye on Blossom Street.

As soon as Harry and Ada had driven off in their car the next day, Snap started to work on his plan. Opening doors was easy for a clever dog like Snap.

He set off down the path and out of the
front gate. He stopped at the bus stop and
stood near a man and a woman.

When the big orange bus came he jumped
on behind them so that the bus driver didn't
notice him. He sat up at the back and
watched out of the window.

Soon they came to Blossom Street and
Snap got off behind a man with a shopping
bag. The driver just saw his tail disappearing.

'Whose dog is that?' he shouted. 'Has
anybody paid for him?' But it was too late.

3

Snap was already running down Blossom
Street. He sniffed at all the doorsteps and the
lamp posts. He chased a cat back on to the
yard wall.

He put his head into Kelly's pram. Kelly
laughed so much that her mum looked to see
what was happening.

'Snap!' she cried in surprise. 'What are you doing here?' Snap wagged his tail and looked hungry.

'Come inside,' said Kelly's mum. 'There's some meat left from yesterday. You can eat that.'

When the children came home from
school they yelled, 'Snap! Snap! We thought
you'd gone for ever.' They patted him and
hugged him. He played with them until they
were called in for tea.

'It's five o'clock,' said Kelly's mum. 'I'd better take Snap back to his new house.' She went to the door and called, 'Snap! Snap!' but Snap was not there. The children looked up and down Blossom Street. But they could not see him. In the end, Kelly's mum set off to Snap's new house.

Ada and Harry were glad to see Kelly's
mum. 'Hello, Irene. It's nice of you to visit
us,' they said.

'I've come about Snap. Oh, he's here!'

'Of course he's here,' said Ada. 'He lives
here. He was fast asleep in the kitchen when
we came home. I think he likes his new
home.'

'Then why was he in Blossom Street all day? I came to tell you,' said Kelly's mum.

'Blossom Street? How could he be? It must be a dog that looks like him,' said Harry.

'Oh no, it was Snap all right. Ask the children.'

'Just come in the other room a minute,'
Ada whispered. 'Snap understands every
word, you know.'

'Rubbish!' said Harry, but he went into the
other room to hear Ada's plan.

'I've got a day off tomorrow,' said Ada. 'I'll
pretend to go to work as usual but I'll hide
and see what he does.'

Next day Ada watched Snap get on the big
orange bus. She wanted to laugh. 'What a
clever dog!' she thought. 'He does
understand.'

She went to Blossom Street and watched
Snap from Kelly's mum's front room.

At half past four Snap trotted off to the
bus stop and caught the bus home. The bus
driver said, 'It's you again, is it?' and let him
on without paying.

When Ada and Harry got home Snap was
curled up, fast asleep. 'No wonder you feel
tired,' said Ada. 'It's hard work looking after
Blossom Street all day.'

Snap pricked up his ears and opened one eye. 'We know all about it, Snap.'

Just then there was a knock on the front door.

'It's a reporter from The Daily Snoop,' said Harry. 'He wants a photo of Snap. The bus driver told him about a clever dog who rides on the bus by himself. More like a naughty dog, I think.'

Snap jumped up and wagged his tail. He liked having his photo taken. The next day everyone in Blossom Street saw him on the front page. The headline said, *Snap goes by bus.*

Lots of people came to ride on the bus with Snap so the bus driver made plenty of money. And Snap is still the boss dog of Blossom Street, even though he doesn't live there any more.

About the author

My name is Rita Ray. I think it is a good name for a writer because people find it easy to remember.

Snap the dog lived in our street when I was a child. He was the boss dog of our street and he really did come back on the bus to keep an eye on things when he moved. Ada, Snap's owner, worked in the sweet factory and she sometimes gave us sweets because we used to give her Snap titbits.

Other Treetops books at this level include:

The Squink by Rita Ray
Jungle Shorts by Irene Rawnsley
Mr Stofflees and the Painted Tiger by Robin Mellor
The Masked Cleaning Ladies of Om by John Coldwell
The Masked Cleaning Ladies Save the Day by John Coldwell

Also available in packs
Stage 10 pack A   0 19 916863 6
Stage 10 class pack A   0 19 916864 4